I DON'T WANT TO GO TO SCHOOL!

by **Lula Bell**

Illustrated by
Brian Fitzgerald

tiger tales

It's my **first day** of school today.

It's my first day
of school today.

I don't want to go!

I don't want to go!

I can't eat my cereal.
I'm SO nervous.

I can't eat
my toast.
I'm SO
nervous.

What if the children don't like me?

What if the teacher doesn't like me?

My heart is beating – ba-DUM, ba-DUM!

My legs are shaking – wibble-wobble!

OH, NO!
The kids look
so **SCARY!**

OH, NO!
The school looks
so **scary!**

**Look at all those sharp
teeth and claws!**

Maybe I'm not the only
one who is **scared.**

Maybe I'm not the only one who is scared.

I will be **brave** if **YOU will** be brave.

What was I so afraid of?

What was I so
afraid of?

This is really fun!

This is really fun!

It's school again tomorrow.

It's school again tomorrow.

And
we . . .